Davy Crockett Gets Hitched

Retold by Bobbi Miller

Illustrated by Megan Lloyd

Holiday House / New York

To Sue and Mark, who inspire me with their perfect dance
—B. M.

To Inness, my sheep-dancing partner,
and Sue, our ovine-canine coach
—M. L.

Library of Congress Cataloging-in-Publication Data
Miller, Bobbi.
Davy Crockett gets hitched / retold by Bobbi Miller ; illustrated by Megan Lloyd. — 1 st ed.
p. cm.
Summary: An accidental encounter with a thorn bush on his way to the spring dance has Davy Crockett
kicking up his heels and out-dancing even the audacious Miss Sally Ann Thunder Ann Whirlwind.
ISBN-13: 978-0-8234-1837-4
1. Crockett, Davy, 1786–1836—Legends. 2. Crockett, Sally Ann Thunder Ann Whirlwind—Legends.
[1. Crockett, Davy, 1786–1836—Legends. 2. Crockett, Sally Ann Thunder Ann Whirlwind—Legends.
3. Folklore—United States. 4. Tall tales.] I. Lloyd, Megan, ill. II. Title.
Pz8.1.M6122Dav 2007
398.2—dc22
[E]
2006050063

SOURCES OF INSPIRATION

Crockett, Davy. *The Adventures of Davy Crockett, Told Mostly by Himself.* New York: Charles
Scribner's Sons, 1934.

Derr, Mark. *The Frontiersman: The Real Life and Many Legends of Davy Crockett.* New York:
William Morrow & Co., Inc., 1993.

Half horse, half alligator, and slightly touched with snapping turtle, Davy Crockett's grin can turn a hailstorm into sunshine. He's whipped his weight in wildcat and hugged many a bear.

Davy was born in the deep woods, a big and wild place with a river
as sassy as a snake. An uncommon big baby, Davy took to growing up
with gumption. By the time he was six years old, he stood as tall as a tree.

By the time he was ten, Davy outhunted every man in the valley. Even the animals passed around word that Davy Crockett was the best of the best. By the time he was full grown, he could outrun a comet, outscreech an eagle, outsneak a raccoon, and outboast a politician.

But his greatest adventure, and certainly one far more painful than every deed he had ever done, began on one fine day of wonderment. That day word spread across the valley that there was going to be a dance. Not just any dance but a spring frolic in honor of Miss Sally Ann Thunder Ann Whirlwind. Full of spit and vinegar, she could run like a shooting star, jump rainbow high, and outwhistle the wind. From all over came the handsome and the not-so-handsome boys to woo the fair Miss Sally Ann.

Always one for a good jig
and a free meal, Davy decided to
see what all the fuss was about.
He took a shortcut through
the woods. Hurrying along,
he backed into a thornbush,
catching a burr in his britches.
With a yelp he ran through the
woods, across the meadow,
straight down to the barn where
the dance was already under way.

Plink, plink, plink! The fiddlers three fiddled out a hearty welcome.
After such a run, Davy thought to sit a spell. Right then that burr
reminded him of the error of his way.

"Yahooo-ooo-ooo-ooo!" he yowled. With a soreful leap,
he jumped into the center of the floor. Miss Sally Ann frowned at the
sight of that dancing wildcat Davy Crockett. No one had ever outdanced
Miss Sally Ann Thunder Ann Whirlwind!

Plink, plink, plink went the fiddlers three. One song ended and another began, not a heartbeat skipped in between. Leaping high and leaping wide, spinning around and around, those handsome and not-so-handsome boys danced, danced, danced. In their midst, Davy outjumped, outtwirled, outyodeled, and outwhirled them all.

And there in the middle of the floor sashayed the splendiferous
Miss Sally Ann. She danced like a streak of lightning buttered with
quicksilver. Davy began to huff and puff. His feet barely touching the
ground, he reeled toward the door; but that burr, still lodged in his
britches, made its point very clear.

"Yahooo-ooo-ooo-ooo!" Davy ballyhooed as he skipped to his Lou.

Plink, plink, plink. The fiddlers three played on through the day and through the night. The moon was so full of itself, it was skipping across the sky in time to the tune. The first of the handsome boys, and one from the not-so-handsome, fell to his knees.

Plink, plink. The fiddlers three became two.

That ripsnorting Davy Crockett bounced higher, reeled faster, and grinned his grinningest best. The kankarriferous burr just wouldn't let loose its bodacious hold.

But that angeliferous Miss Sally Ann, she was not pleased at all. No one outdanced her, not if she had anything to do about it!

That soft-peach Miss Sally Ann grinned right back at him. With a one-two-THREE step, she whirlijigged by the vittles table. With a swing of her skirt, she toppled the vat of churned butter, greasing the floor mightily fine.

Down went a handsome boy, and a not-so-handsome boy,
in a heap of arms and legs. But not Davy Crockett.
"YAHOO!" he shouted louder than the lot,
the burr jumping like a bean. He kicked the
doves out of the rafters.

You just know that sweet-plum Miss Sally Ann was getting more than a little worried now. She waltzed to the pickle barrel and toppled it over. Garlic pickles rolled across the floor. *Plop, plop* went a handsome boy, and a not-so-handsome boy.

"Yahooo-ooo-ooo-ooo!" Davy warbled, that burr having a mind of its own. Good thing garlic pickles were his favorite. He was working up a voraciferous hunger.

Miss Sally Ann hoofed her way to the barrel of apples and gave a gentle nudge. *Plikity, plikity,* apples rambled across the floor.

"Yahooo-ooo!" As the burr tromped, Davy stomped, turning the apples into applesauce.

She high-stepped to the stack of potatoes and gave a good wallop.
Plunk, plunk. Potatoes rolled along the floor.

"Yahooo-ooo!" As the burr gnashed, Davy mashed, making
them potatoes into a fine delight.

Then Miss Sally Ann caught the lace tablecloth and gave
a slight yank. Corncobs flew, pea pods too. Carrots skirred,
turnips whirred. Chicken was dumped; flapjacks were flipped.

"Yahooo-ooo!" Davy grinned an uncommon fine grin. With a whirl and a swirl, all thanks to that burr, he stirred up some mighty fine chicken and dumpling stew. Potato dumplings, of course. Even Miss Sally Ann was duly impressed. She gave the most toothiferous smile, pretty as you please.

"Yahooo-ooo-ooo-ooo!" Davy's melodious measure rang high in delight. Seems as if with all that shaking going on, that burr in his britches finally dislodged, and moved to a less spiteful location.

"You serve a mighty fine supper," he sang. "The finest I've ever taken the pleasure to partake!"

Plink. The fiddlers two became one.

By morning light the last fiddler burned the last of his strings. Two dancers stomped the floor. Having forgotten the burr, that rambunctious Davy saw only the gleam in Miss Sally Ann's eye, and that was enough to keep him dancing. And that sweetly thing Miss Sally Ann finally found her match, and that was enough to keep her dancing.

By the time the sun do-si-doed with the moon that night, they were
wed: Davy and Mrs. Sally Ann Thunder Ann Whirlwind Crockett.